Party Time

by Ruth Mattison

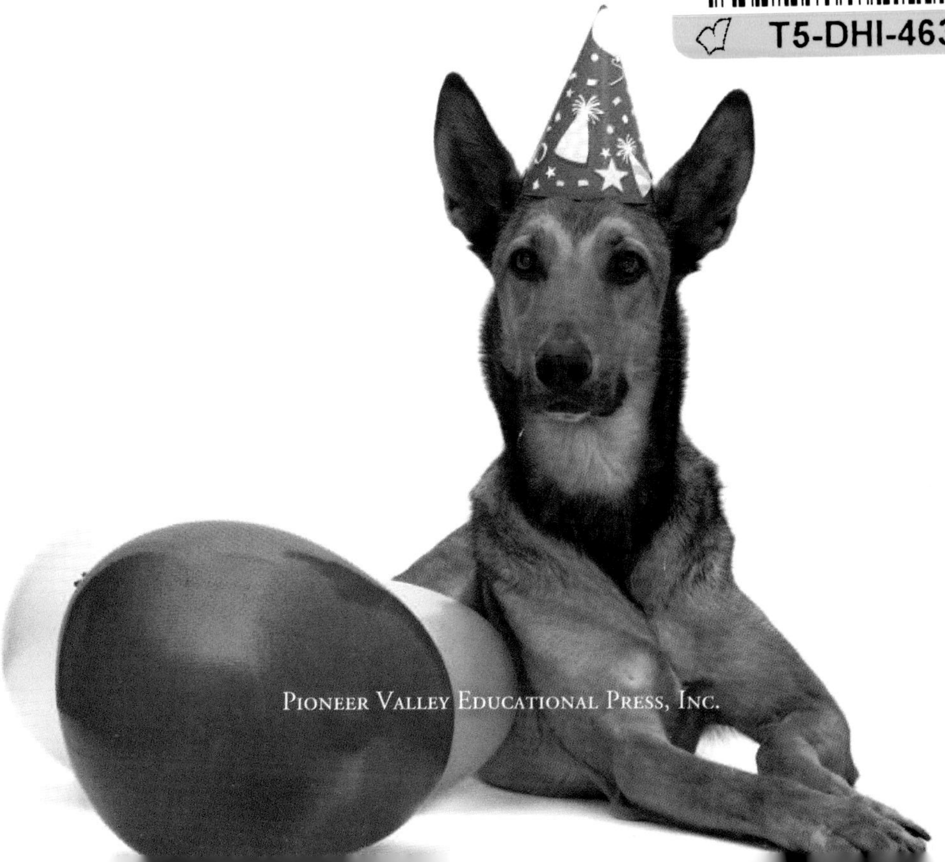

Pioneer Valley Educational Press, Inc.

"Look at me!
I am going to a party."

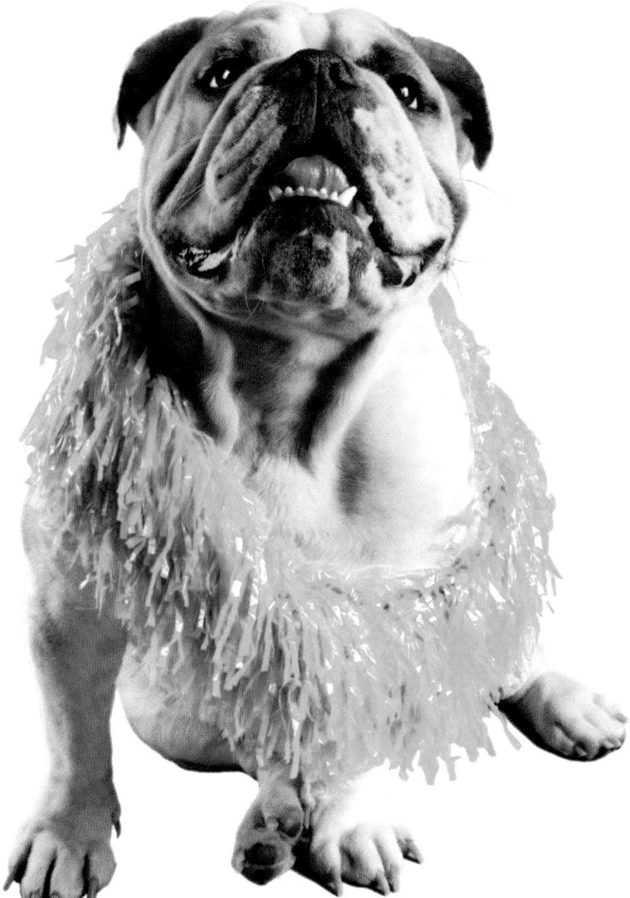

Can I come?

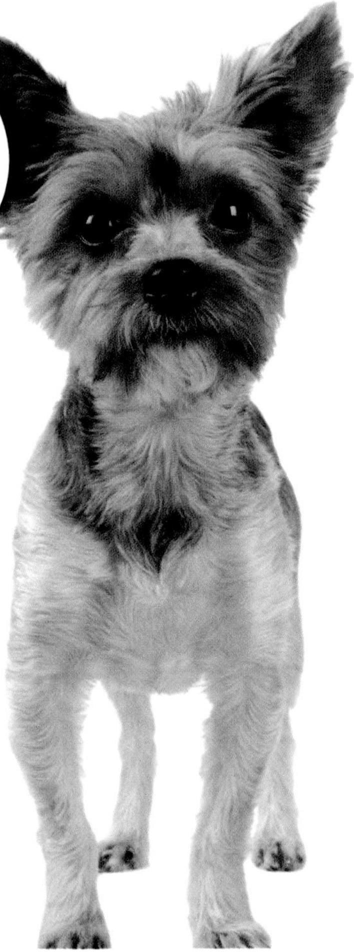

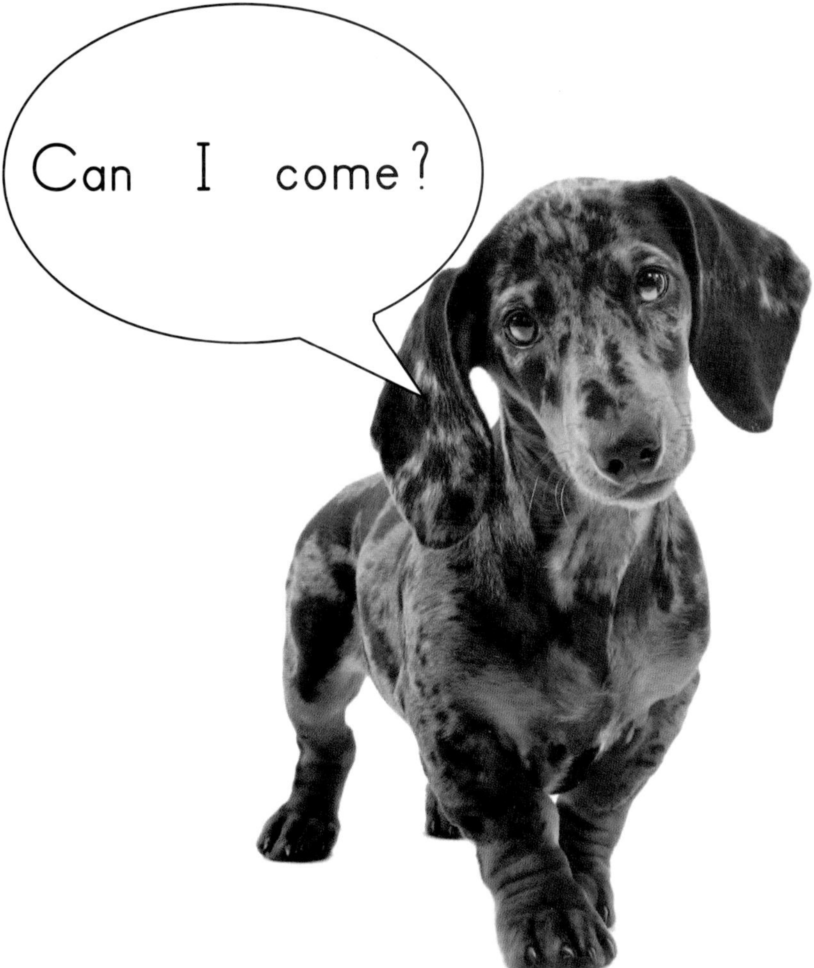
Can I come?

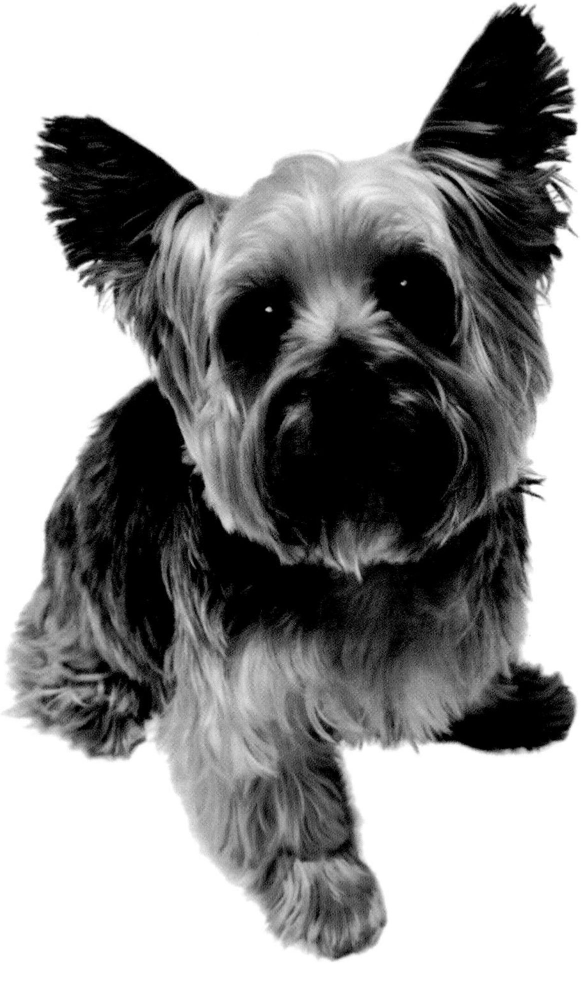

Can I come, too?

Can we come?

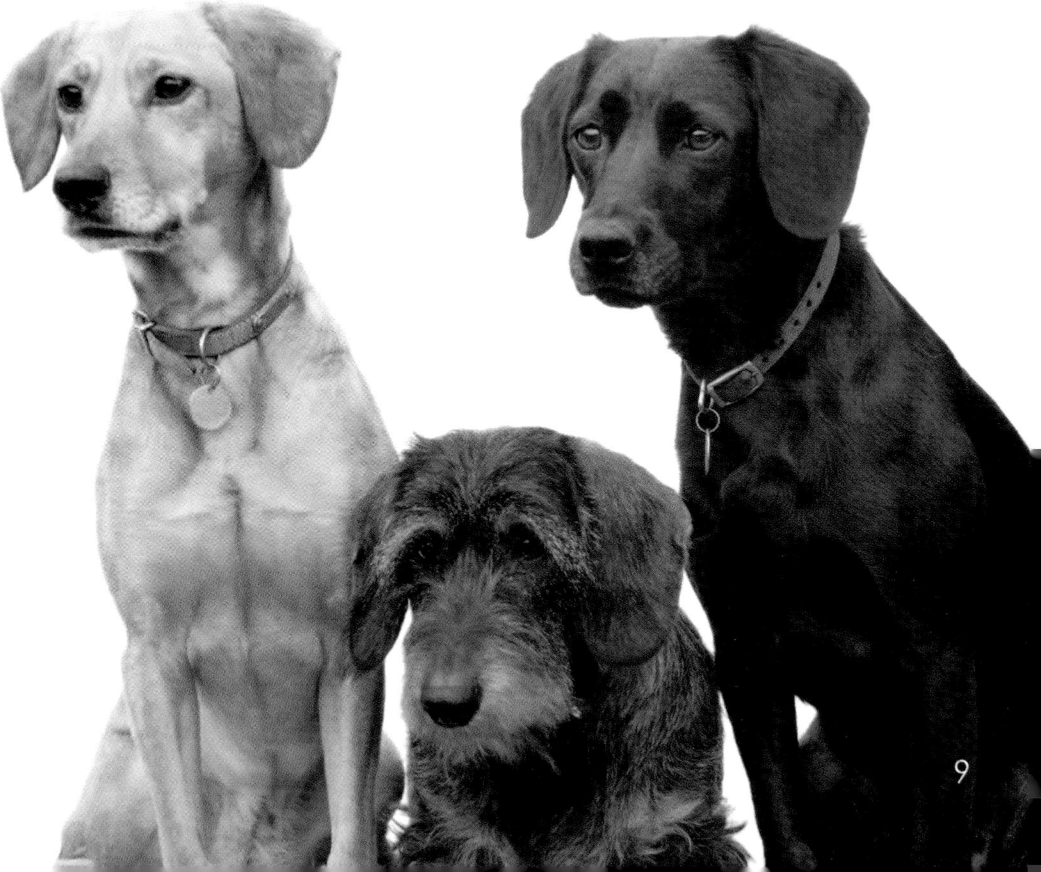

Yes! Come on!

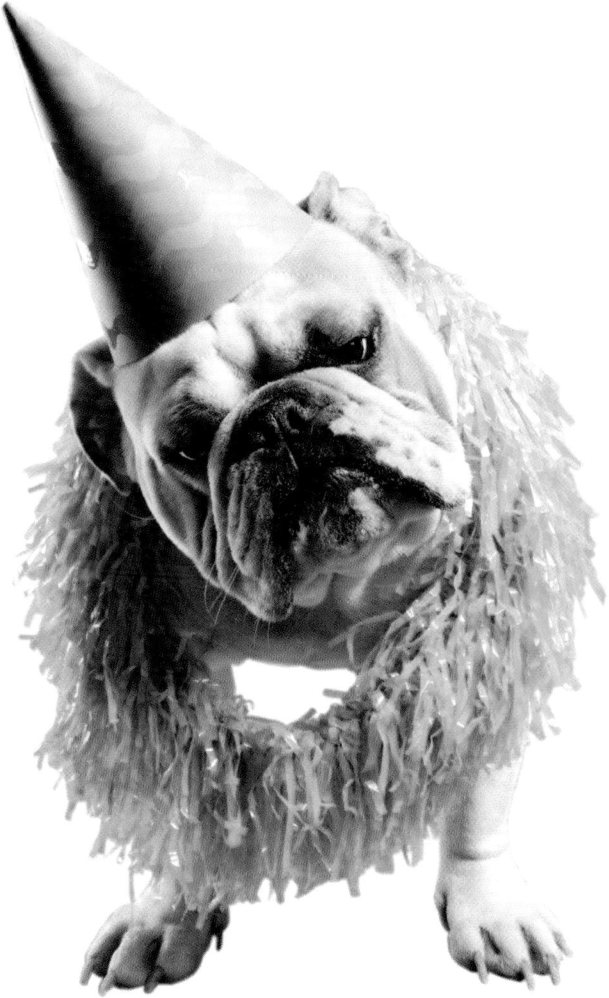

"Come to the dog party!"

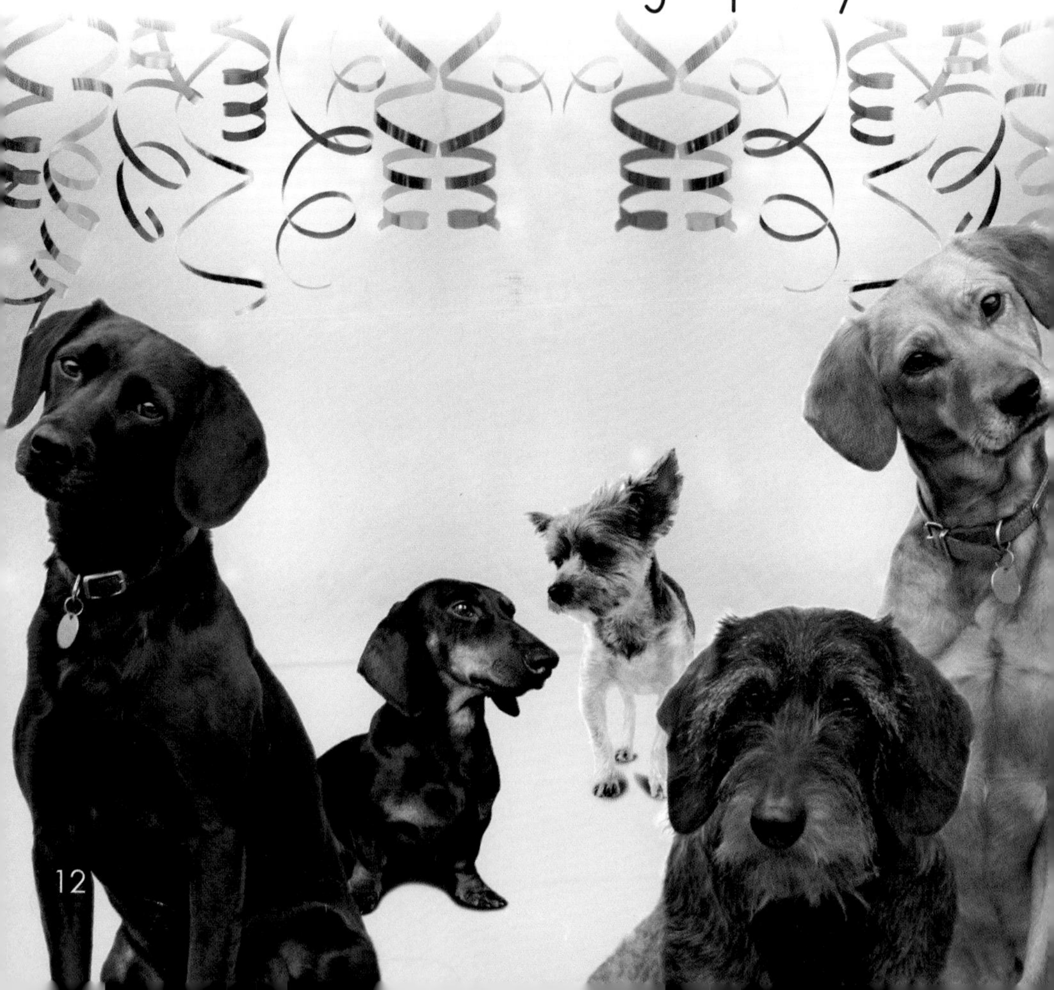